DANIEL'S GREAT ADVENTURES!

BOOK ONE: DANIEL IS BAPTIZED

Written by: **Miriam Nabil Agaybi**

Illustrated by: **Sandi Banna**

Today is a very special day.

Today baby Daniel is 40 days old!

Daniel's mom and dad are all ready to go to church,

because today
is Daniel's
baptismal day!

4

Abouna is so excited to baptize Daniel.

Abouna starts by praying the absolution for mom and anoints her with holy oil.

Next, mom carries baby Daniel with her left arm and casts off the devil with her right hand, saying, "I renounce you, Satan."

After Abouna blesses the water, he puts baby Daniel in the water, 3 times. In the name of the Father, the Son, and the Holy Spirit.

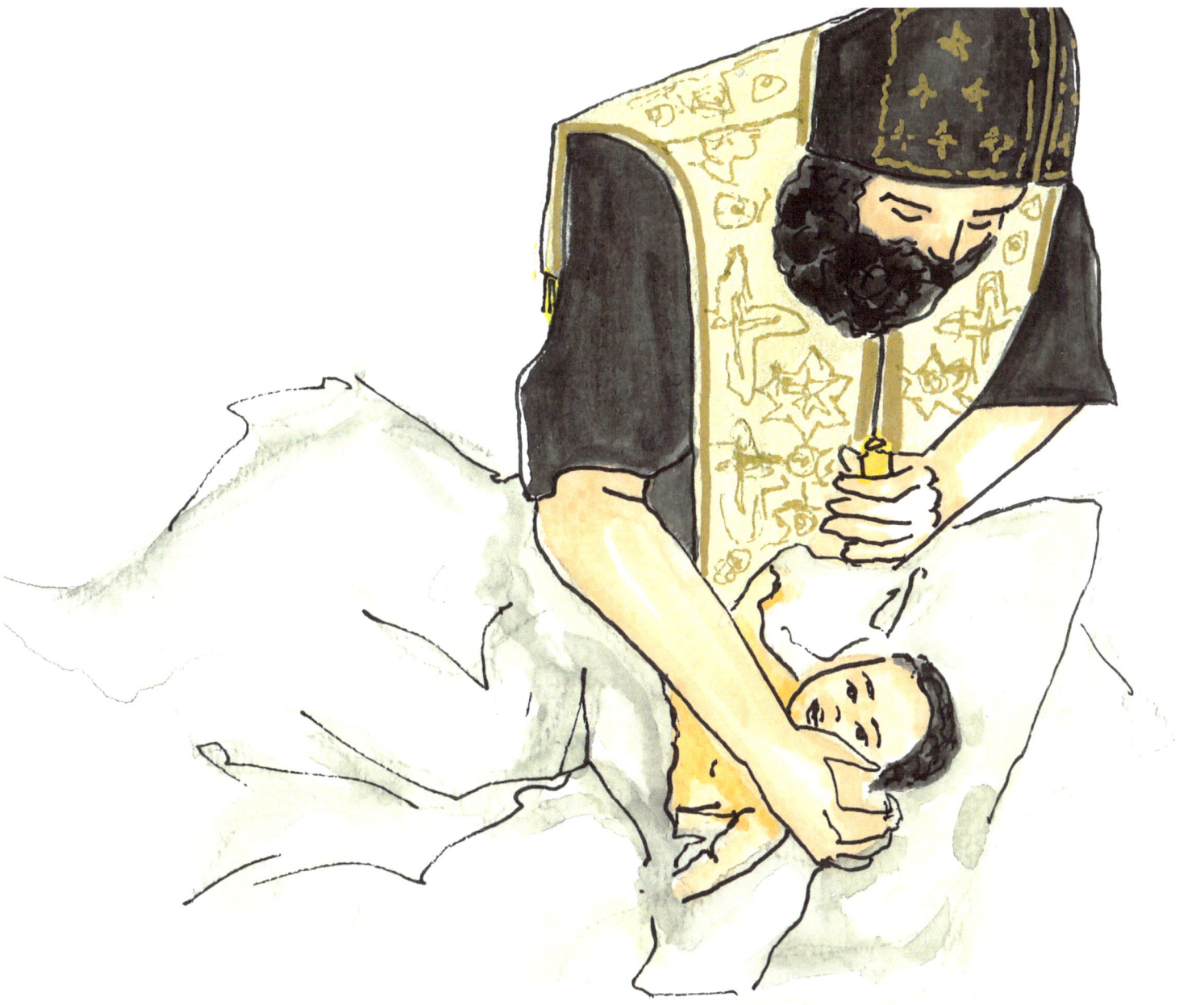

When Abouna takes him out of the water, he anoints him with the holy myron oil, 36 times!

Baby Daniel is dressed in beautiful white clothes and a red ribbon.

Now he can take communion!

Dad and mom walk around the whole church carrying Daniel, as the congregation chants with joy.

Abouna says a prayer and then takes the red ribbon off.

14

The whole congregation is full of joy!

Everyone is so joyful, including baby Daniel!

"Jesus answered, "Most assuredly, I say to you, unless one is born of water ...

... and the Spirit, he cannot enter the kingdom of God."

— John 3:5